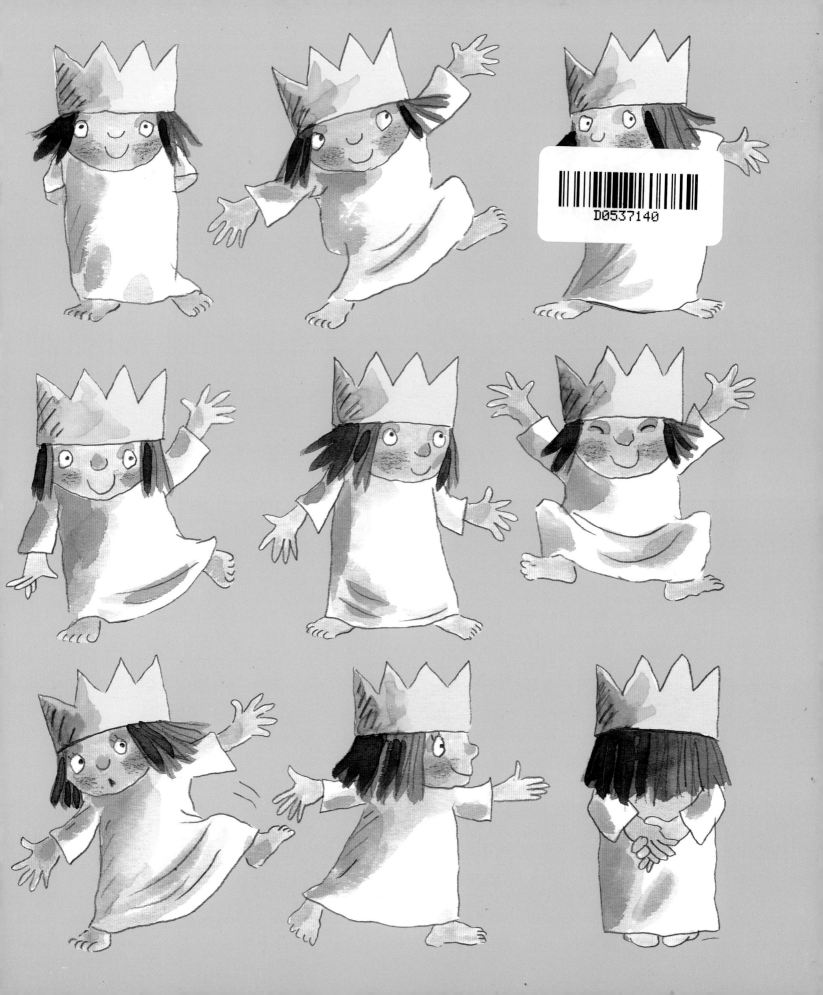

American edition published in 2016 by Andersen Press USA,

an imprint of Andersen Press Ltd.

www.andersenpressusa.com

First published in Great Britain in 2016 by Andersen Press Ltd.,

20 Vauxhall Bridge Road, London SW1V 2SA.

Distributed in the United States and Canada by

Lerner Publishing Group, Inc.

241 First Avenue North

Minneapolis, MN 55401 USA

For reading levels and more information, look up this title at www.lernerbooks.com.

Color separated in Switzerland by Photolitho AG, Zürich.

Printed and bound in China.

Library of Congress Cataloging-in-Publication Data Available.

ISBN: 978-1-5124-1629-9

eBook ISBN: 978-1-5124-1632-9

1-TL-6/1/16

A Little Princess Story

I Want a Bedtime Story!

Tony Ross

Andersen Press USA

Every bedtime, the King told the Little Princess a story.
But one night he was away on royal business, so the Queen
told the Little Princess a story about a fairy queen.

"That's not as good as Daddy's story," said the Little Princess, and she wouldn't go to sleep.

So the Admiral told the Little Princess a story
about the high seas and the giant fish who lived there.

"That's not as good as Daddy's story!" said the Little Princess,
and she still wouldn't go to sleep.

So then the General told the Little Princess a story
about a great battle, where everybody ran away.

"That's not as good as Daddy's story!" said the Little Princess, and she still absolutely would not go to sleep.

So next the Cook told the Little Princess a story about a really naughty sandwich.

"That's not as good as Daddy's story!" said the Little Princess, and she still, absolutely, positively would not go to sleep.

The Prime Minister told a story about his big nose and the
Gardener told one about a carrot that was afraid of the dark…

… but NOBODY could tell a story as well as the King.
"I want a bedtime story!" cried the Little Princess.
Everybody looked at the maid. "She wants a story!" they all cried.

"I don't know any stories," said the Maid, "but I DO have an idea."
Taking the Little Princess by the hand, she led her downstairs,
then down some more stairs…

… and down even more stairs, along a passage,
to a door marked LIBRARY.

The Maid flung open the door. "Here you are," she cried,
"all the stories you need!" The Little Princess blinked.
"These aren't stories," she said, "they're books."

"The stories are IN the books!" said the Maid, taking one off the nearest shelf. "Look, you can read one for yourself."

"I can't read a whole book," said the Little Princess.
"You CAN read some of the little words," said the Maid,
"and the pictures will help you to tell the story."

The Little Princess grabbed a book. She liked the shiny cover,
she liked the colorful pictures, she liked turning the pages
and working out the secrets of the words.

Soon she was running up and down the library shelves,
taking this book, that book, then another book, until
the Maid was weighed down with a huge pile.

Back in bed, the Little Princess sat surrounded by books.
Her favorite one had belonged to her daddy when
he was a little prince. It was all about bears.

"THIS IS DADDY'S STORY!" the Little Princess cried in delight.
She had heard it so many times, she knew exactly what
the secret words said. She read it over and over again.

"Nighty night, sleepy tight, time to turn off the light," said the Maid. "Wait!" said the Little Princess. "When I've finished Daddy's story…"

"... I want to read all these too!"

CLICK!

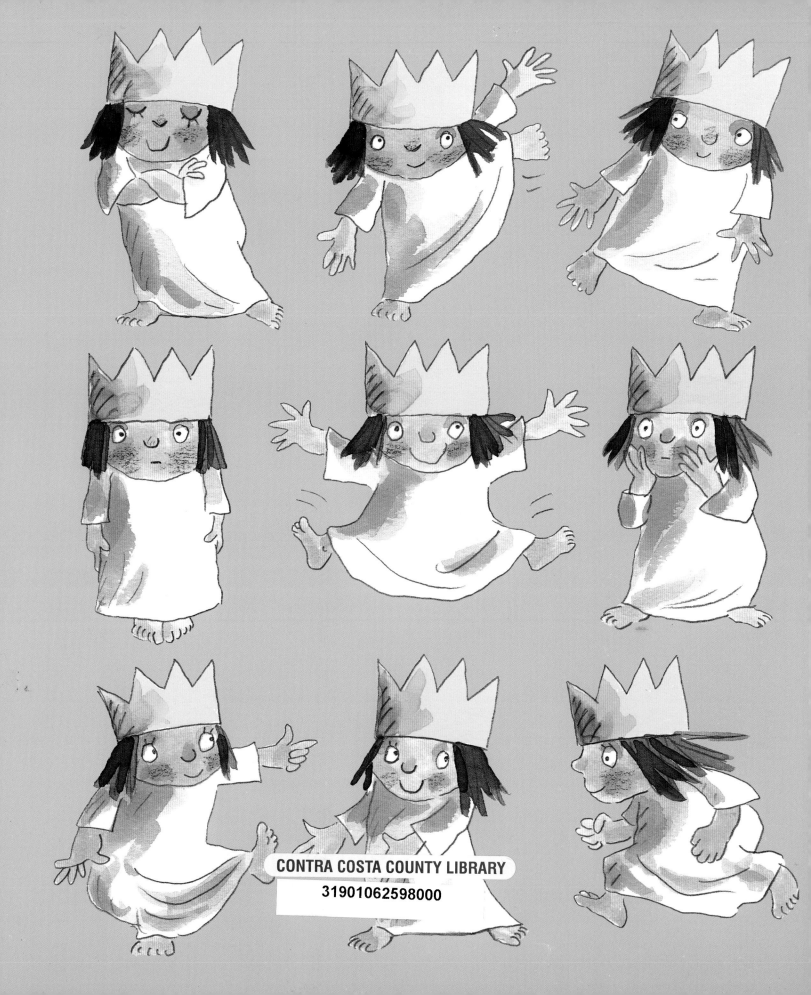